Something Drastic

chocolate

Poems by Michael Rosen

Illustrations by Tim Archbold

Collins

Contents

Late Last Night

Late last night
I lay in bed
driving buses
in my head.

Don't

Don't do,
Don't do,
Don't do that.
Don't pull faces,
Don't tease the cat.

Don't pick your ears,
Don't be rude at school.
Who do they think I am?

Some kind of fool?

One day
they'll say,
Don't put toffee in my coffee,
don't pour gravy on the baby,
don't put beer in his ear,
don't stick your toes up his nose.

Don't put confetti on the spaghetti
and don't squash peas on your knees.

Don't put ants in your pants,
don't put mustard in the custard,

don't chuck jelly at the telly

and don't throw fruit at a computer,
don't throw fruit at a computer.

Don't what?
Don't throw fruit at a computer.
Don't what?
Don't throw fruit at a computer.
Who do they think I am?
Some kind of fool?

Something's Drastic

Something's drastic
my nose is made of plastic
something's drastic
my ears are elastic
something's drastic
something's drastic.
I'm fantastic!

The Hidebehind

Have you seen the Hidebehind?
I don't think you will, mind you,
because as you're running through the dark
the Hidebehind's behind you.

The Car Trip

Mum says:
"Right, you two,
this is a very long car journey.
I want you two to be good.
I'm driving and I can't drive properly
if you two are going mad in the back.
Do you understand?"

So we say,
"OK, Mum, OK. Don't worry,"
and off we go.

And we start The Moaning:
Can I have a drink?
I want some crisps.
Can I open my window?
He's got my book.
Get off me.
Ow, that's my ear!

And Mum tries to be exciting:
"Look out the window,
there's a lamp post."

And we go on with The Moaning:
Can I have a sweet?
He's sitting on me.
Are we nearly there?
Don't scratch.
You never tell him off.
Now he's biting his nails.
I want a drink. I want a drink.

And Mum tries to be exciting again:
"Look out the window,
there's a tree."

And we go on:

My hands are sticky.

He's playing with the door handle now.

I feel sick.

Your nose is all runny.

Don't pull my hair.

He's punching me, Mum,

That's really dangerous, you know.

Mum, he's spitting.

And Mum says:

"Right, I'm stopping the car.

I AM STOPPING THE CAR."

She stops the car.

"Now, if you two don't stop it

I'm going to put you out the car

and leave you by the side of the road."

He started it.
I didn't. He started it.

"I don't care who started it.
I can't drive properly
if you two go mad in the back.
Do you understand?"

And we say:
"OK, Mum, OK, don't worry."

"Can I have a drink?"

Down Behind The Dustbin

Down behind the dustbin
I met a dog called Mary.
"I wish I wasn't a dog," she said,
"I wish I was a canary."

Down behind the dustbin
I met a dog called Joe.
"What have you got there?" I said.
"Wouldn't you like to know?"

12

Down behind the dustbin
I met a dog called Jim.
He didn't know me
and I didn't know him.

Down behind the dustbin
I met a dog called Felicity.
"It's a bit dark here," she said,
"They've cut off the electricity."

13

Hey Diddle Diddle

Hey diddle diddle,
The cat and the fiddle,
The cow jumped over the moon.
The little dog laughed
To see such fun,
And the dish ran away with the chocolate biscuits.

14

Tough Guy

I'm the big sleeper
rolled up in his sheets
at the break of the day.

I'm a big sleeper living soft
in a hard kind of way

the light through the curtain
can't wake me
I'm under the blankets
you can't shake me
the pillow rustler

and blanket gambler
a mean tough eiderdown man.

I keep my head
I stay in bed.

Round The Park

Where are you going?
  Round the park.
When are you back?
  After dark.

Won't you be scared?
  What a laugh.
A ghost'll get you.
  Don't be daft.

I know where it lives.
  No you don't.
And you'll run away.
  No I won't.

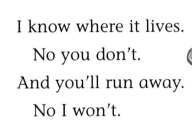

It got me once.
　　It didn't … did it?
It's all SLIMY.
　　Tisn't … is it?

Where are you going?
　　I'm staying at home.
Aren't you going to the park?
　　Not on my own.

Rodge Said

Rodge said,
"Teachers – they want it all ways –
You're jumping up and down on a chair
or something
and they grab hold of you and say,
'Would you do that sort of thing in your own home?'

"So you say, 'No.'
And they say,
'Well don't do it here then.'

"But if you say, 'Yes, I do it at home.'
they say,
'Well, we don't want that sort of thing
going on here
thank you very much.'

"Teachers – they get you all ways,"
Rodge said.

Say Please

I'll have a please sandwich cheese.

No I mean a knees sandwich please.

Sorry I mean a fleas sandwich please.

No, a please sandwich please,

No   No –

I'll have a doughnut.

Going Through The Old Photos

Who's that?
That's your Auntie Mabel
and that's me
under the table.

Who's that?
That's Uncle Billy.
Who's that?
Me being silly.

Who's that
licking a lolly?
I'm not sure
but I think it's Polly.

Who's that
behind the tree?
I don't know,
I can't see.
Could be you,
Could be me.

Who's that?
Baby Joe.
Who's that?
I don't know.

Who's that standing
on his head?
Turn it round.
It's Uncle Ted.

21

Newcomers

My father came to England
from another country.
My father's mother came to England
from another country,
but my father's father
stayed behind.

So my dad had no dad here
and I never saw him at all.

One day in spring
some things arrived:
a few old papers,
a few old photos
and – oh yes –
a hulky bulky thick checked jacket
that belonged to the man
I would have called "Grandad".
The Man Who Stayed Behind.

But I kept that jacket
and I wore it
and I wore it
and I wore it
till it wore right through
at the back.

When We Go Over To My Grandad's

When we go over
to my grandad's,
he falls asleep.

While he's asleep,
he snores.

When he wakes up,
he says,
"Did I snore?
Did I snore?
Did I snore?"

Everybody says, "No,
you didn't snore."

Why do we lie to him?

Look - Said The Boy

Look – said the boy
the scaffold-man at work
is like a spider on his net.

No – said the scaffold-man
I'm just a fly
in the trap the spider set.

The Itch

If your hands get wet
in the washing-up water,
if they get covered in flour,
if you get grease or oil
all over your fingers,
if they land up in the mud,
wet grit, paint, or glue …

have you noticed
it's just then
that you always get
a terrible itch
just inside your nose?

And you can try to
twitch your nose,
twist your nose,
squeeze your nose,
scratch it with your arm,
scrape your nose on
your shoulder

or press it
up against the wall,
but it's no good.
You can't get rid of
the itch.
It drives you so mad
you just have to let
a finger get at it.

And before you know
you've done it.
You've wiped a load of glue,
or oil,
or cold wet pastry
all over the end of your nose.

Quiet Please

No need to shout
no need to yell
no need to have a riot.
Shut your eyes
take a deep breath —
Ooh, you've gone all quiet!

The Hardest Thing To Do In The World

The hardest thing to do in the world
is stand in the hot sun
at the end of a long queue for ice creams
watching all the people who've just bought theirs
coming away from the queue
giving their ice creams their very first lick.

A feelings wheel

Late last night
I lay in bed
driving buses
in my head.

The little dog laughed
To see such fun,
And the dish ran away with
   the chocolate biscuits.

I'm fantastic!

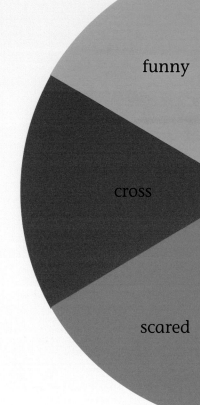

funny

cross

scared

I'm a big sleeper living soft
in a hard kind of way

Where are you going?
   I'm staying at home.
Aren't you going to the park?
   Not on my own.

"Right, I'm stopping the car.
I AM STOPPING THE CAR."

Don't put ants in your pants,
don't put mustard in the custard,

And we go on with The Moaning:
Can I have a sweet?
He's sitting on me.
Are we nearly there?

happy

thoughtful

No – said the scaffold-man
I'm just a fly
in the trap the spider set.

bored

I'll have a please sandwich cheese.

Everybody says, "No,
you didn't snore."
Why do we lie to him?

Ideas for guided reading

Learning objectives: compare and contrast poems on similar themes; select, prepare, read aloud and recite by heart poetry; recognise rhyme, alliteration and other patterns of sound that create effects; identify common punctuation marks and respond to them appropriately when reading; comment constructively on plays and performance

Curriculum links: ICT: Combining text and graphics; Music: Play it again – Exploring rhythmic patterns

Interest words: confetti, rustler, eiderdown, scaffold, queue

Resources: whiteboards or scrap paper and a pencil/felt pen

Getting started

This book can be read over two or more guided reading sessions.

- Open a discussion with the statement: *Good poems rhyme.* Ask the children if they agree or disagree. Introduce this book of poetry by Michael Rosen. Do the children know any other books written by Michael Rosen? (E.g. *We're Going on a Bear Hunt!*)

- Explain that this poet uses rhyme, but not all the time. *What other features of language do poets use when they don't use rhyme?* Make a list of these (e.g. *alliteration, assonance, repetition, metaphor, punctuation*).

- Look at p2 and as a group, choose a few poems to read including 'Down Behind the Dustbin', 'Tough Guy' and 'Newcomers'.

Reading and responding

- Ask them to read each poem silently, then discuss thoughts and opinions as a group. Encourage personal responses such as, *I liked that one because…* or *That one was unusual because…*

- Ask volunteers to read aloud while others evaluate the expression and phrasing used. Check that punctuation is observed to achieve the correct rhythm.

- Ask them to make a note of the language features they notice by referring to the list made earlier.